# A Few Lessons
# From Sherlock Holmes

## Peter Bevelin

Paperback ISBN 9781780924489
ePub ISBN 9781780924496
PDF ISBN  9781780924502

Published in the UK by MX Publishing
335 Princess Park Manor, Royal Drive,
London, N11 3GX
www.mxpublishing.co.uk
Cover design by www.staunch.com

# INTRODUCTION

## Characters

Arthur Conan Doyle – Scottish physician and writer, most remembered for his stories about the detective Sherlock Holmes (1859 – 1930)

Joseph Bell – Scottish professor of clinical surgery (1837 – 1911) and Doyle's inspiration for Sherlock Holmes

Sherlock Holmes – A London-based fictional detective

Dr. John Watson – A fictional character and Holmes's assistant

C. Auguste Dupin – A fictional detective in stories by Edgar Allan Poe (1809 – 1849)

Dr. John Evelyn Thorndyke – A fictional detective and forensic scientist in stories by R. Austin Freeman (1862 – 1943)

Francis Bacon – English scientist and philosopher (1561 – 1626)

Claude Bernard – French physiologist (1813 – 1878)

Aulus Cornelius Celsus – Roman encyclopedist, known for his extant medical work (25 BC – ca 50)

Jean-Martin Charcot – French neurologist and professor of pathology (1825 – 1893)

Georges Cuvier – French naturalist and zoologist (1769 – 1832)

Charles Robert Darwin – English naturalist and writer (1809 – 1882)

Benjamin Jowett – British classical scholar (1817 – 1893)

James Alexander Lindsay – Irish professor of medicine (1856 – 1931)

Thomas McCrae – American professor of medicine and colleague of Sir William Osler (1870 – 1935)

Michel de Montaigne – French statesman and author (1533 – 1592)

William Osler – Canadian physician (1849 –1919)

Louis Pasteur – French chemist and microbiologist (1822 – 1895)

Charles Sanders Peirce – American scientist and philosopher (1839 – 1914)

Oliver Wendell Holmes, Sr. – American physician and author (1809 – 1894)

## Some background

### Dr. Joseph Bell was the inspiration for Arthur Conan Doyle

*The most notable of the characters whom I met was one Joseph Bell, surgeon at the Edinburgh Infirmary. Bell was a very remarkable man in body and mind...He was a very skillful surgeon, but his strong point was diagnosis, not only of disease, but of occupation and character...I had ample chance of studying his methods....It is no wonder that after the study of such character I used and amplified his methods when in later life I tried to build up a scientific detective who solved cases on his own merits and not through the folly of the criminal. (A.C. Doyle; Memories and Adventures)*

*Sherlock Holmes is the literary embodiment, if I may so express it, of my memory of a professor of medicine at Edinburgh University. (A.C. Doyle; Teller of Tales)*

*I thought of my old teacher Joe Bell, of his eagle face, of his curious ways of his eerie trick of spotting details. If he were a detective he would surely reduce this fascinating business to something nearer an exact science. I would try it if I could get this effect. (A.C. Doyle; Memories and Adventures)*

### In a letter to Dr. Bell, Doyle wrote

*It is most certainly to you that I owe Sherlock Holmes, and though in the stories I have the advantage of being able to place [the detective] in all sorts of dramatic positions, I do not think that his analytical work is in the least an exaggeration of some effects which I have* seen you produce in the out-patient ward. *Round the centre of deduction and inference and observation which I heard you inculate I have tried to build up a man who pushed the things as far as it would go - further occasionally - and I am so glad that the result has satisfied you, who are the critic with the most right to be severe.* (Joseph Bell; *Dr. Joe Bell*)

## Dr. Bell wrote on Doyle
*I always regarded him as one of the best students I ever had. He was exceedingly interested always upon anything connected with diagnosis, and was never tired of trying to discover all those little details which one looks for.* (Joseph Bell; *Joseph Bell: An Appreciation by an Old Friend*)

## The reader may wonder why I involve quotes from medicine. Professor Bell may provide an answer
*The experienced physician and the trained surgeon every day, in their examinations of the humblest patient, have to go through a similar process of reasoning, quick or slow according to the personal equations of each, almost automatic in the experienced man, laboured and often erratic in the tyro, yet requiring just the same simple requisites, senses to notice facts, and education and intelligence to apply them.* (Dr. Joseph Bell; *The Bookman*)

*Dr. Conan Doyle's education as a student of medicine taught him how to observe, and his practice, both as a general practitioner and a specialist, has been a splendid training for a man such as he is, gifted with eyes, memory, and imagination. Eyes and ears which* can see and hear, memory to record at once and to recall at pleasure the impressions of the senses, and an imagination capable of weaving a theory or piecing together a broken chain or unraveling a tangled clue, such are implements of his trade to a successful diagnostician. (Dr. Joseph Bell; *The Bookman*)

## Medical Professor McCrae adds
*We have such problems as part of our daily task and our work may be regarded as much like that of the criminal detective. He has a general knowledge of the members of the criminal class; we of disease in general. He knows that certain men have certain methods of work; we know the features of special diseases. It is stated that the police can classify habitual criminals more or less by their methods and, knowing the men in their city who work in a particular way, can narrow down the possibilities of a given crime to a few men. This may be described as the natural history of crime. So, too, we in medicine narrow down the possibilities.* (Thomas McCrae; *The Method of Zadig*)

## I have only one ambition and I cherish no greater hope than that of being useful. So let the journey begin
*The general lines of reasoning advocated by Holmes have a real practical application to life.* (A.C. Doyle; *Memories and Adventures*)

*It has always been my habit to hide none of my methods, either from my friend Watson or from anyone who might take an intelligent interest in them.* (Holmes; *The Reigate Squire*)

## SOME LESSONS

**What distinguishes Holmes from most mortals is that he knows where to look and what questions to ask. He pays attention to the important things and he knows where to find them.**

### Mathematics and science writer Martin Gardner on Sherlock Holmes

*Like the scientist trying to solve a mystery of nature, Holmes first gathered all the evidence he could that was relevant to his problem. At times, he performed experiments to obtain fresh data. He then surveyed the total evidence in the light of his vast knowledge of crime, and/or sciences relevant to crime, to arrive at the most probable hypothesis. Deductions were made from the hypothesis; then the theory was further tested against new evidence, revised if need be, until finally the truth emerged with a probability close to certainty.* (Martin Gardner)

### Holmes on necessary qualities for good detective work

*I was consulted last week by Francois le Villard, who, as you probably know, has come rather to the front lately in the French detective service...He possesses two out of the three qualities necessary for the ideal detective. He has the power of observation and that of deduction. He is only wanting in knowledge, and that may come in time.* (Holmes; *The Sign of the Four*)

**To know what to do and not do, we first need some genuine understanding on how reality is – how things and people are and what works and not**

*When I first came up to London I had rooms in Montague Street, just round the corner from the British Museum, and there I waited, filling in my too abundant leisure time by studying all those branches of science which might make me more efficient.* (Holmes; *The Musgrave Ritual*)

*He [Holmes] appears to have a passion for definite and exact knowledge.* (Stamford, old friend of Dr. Watson; *A Study in Scarlet*)

*I have a lot of special knowledge which I apply to the problem, and which facilitates matters wonderfully.* (Holmes; *A Study in Scarlet*)

*His zeal for certain studies was remarkable, and within eccentric limits his knowledge was so extraordinarily ample and minute that his observations have fairly astounded me.* (Dr. Watson; *A Study in Scarlet*)

**Considering many ideas over a wide range of disciplines give us perspective and help us consider the big picture or many aspects of an issue**

*Breadth of view...is one of the essentials of our profession. The interplay of ideas and the oblique uses of knowledge are often of extraordinary interest.* (Holmes; *The Valley of Fear*)

*One's ideas must be as broad as Nature if they are to interpret Nature.* (Holmes; *A Study in Scarlet*)

*Our divisions into sciences are not a part of nature...in nature there is really neither chemistry nor physics, nor zoology, nor physiology, nor pathology; there are only bodies to be classified or phenomena to be known and mastered.* (Claude Bernard)

*He [Mycroft; Holmes brother] has the tidiest and most orderly brain, with the greatest capacity for storing facts, of any man living...The conclusions of every department are passed to him, and he is the central exchange, the clearinghouse, which makes out the balance. All other men are specialists, but his specialism is omniscience. We will suppose that a minister needs information as to a point which involves the Navy, India, Canada and the bimetallic question; he could get his separate advices from various departments upon each, but only Mycroft can focus them all, and say offhand how each factor would affect the other.* (Holmes; *The Bruce-Partington Plans*)

## But only what is useful – it can be dangerous to know too much

*He [Doyle] created a shrewd, quick-sighted, inquisitive man...with plenty of spare time, a retentive memory, and perhaps with the best gift of all – the power of unloading the mind of all burden of trying to remember unnecessary details.* (Dr. Joseph Bell; *The Bookman*)

*His ignorance was as remarkable as his knowledge...He said that he would acquire no knowledge which did not bear upon his object.*

9

*Therefore all the knowledge which he possessed was such as would be useful to him.* (Dr. Watson; *A Study in Scarlet*)

*It is not so impossible...that a man should possess all knowledge which is likely to be useful to him in his work.* (Holmes; *The Five Orange Pips*)

*I consider that a man's brain originally is like a little empty attic, and you have to stock it with such furniture as you choose. A fool takes in all the lumber of every sort that he comes across, so that the knowledge which might be useful to him gets crowded out, or at best is jumbled up with a lot of other things so that he has a difficulty in laying his hands upon it.* (Holmes; *A Study in Scarlet*)

*Now the skillful workman is very careful indeed as to what he takes into his brain-attic. He will have nothing but the tools which may help him in doing his work, but of these he has a large assortment, and all in the most perfect order. It is a mistake to think that that little room has elastic walls and can distend to any extent. Depend upon it there comes a time when for every addition of knowledge you forget something that you knew before. It is of the highest importance, therefore, not to have useless facts elbowing out the useful ones.* (Holmes; *A Study in Scarlet*)

*I say now, as I said then, that a man should keep his little brain-attic stocked with all the furniture that he is likely to use, and the rest he can put away in the lumber-room of his library, where he can get it if he wants it.* (Holmes; *The Five Orange Pips*)

**It is useful to know something about human nature and what motivates people**

*Human nature is a strange mixture, Watson. You see that even a villain and murderer can inspire such affection that his brother turns to suicide when he learns that his neck is forfeited.* (Holmes; *The Stock-Broker's Clerk*)

*The old story, Watson. A treacherous friend and a fickle wife.* (Holmes; *The Retired Colourman*)

*He is the king of all the blackmailers. Heaven help the man, and still more the woman, whose secret and reputation come into the power of Milverton! With a smiling face and a heart of marble, he will squeeze and squeeze until he has drained them dry.* (Holmes; *Charles Augustus Milverton*)

*Work is the best antidote to sorrow, my dear Watson...and I have a piece of work for us both to-night which, if we can bring it to a successful conclusion, will in itself justify a man's life on this planet.* (Holmes; *The Empty House*)

*My dear Watson, you as a medical man are continually gaining light as to the tendencies of a child by the study of the parents. Don't you see that the converse is equally valid? I have frequently gained my first real insight into the character of parents by studying their children.* (Holmes; *The Copper Beeches*)

*When a woman thinks that her house is on fire, her instinct is at once to rush to the thing which she values most. It is a perfectly overpowering impulse...A married woman grabs at her baby—an unmarried one reaches for her jewel box.* (Holmes; *A Scandal in Bohemia*)

*Jealousy is a strange transformer of characters.* (Holmes; *The Noble Bachelor*)

*There can be no doubt that Stapleton exercised an influence over her which may have been love or may have been fear, or very possibly both, since they are by no means incompatible emotions.* (Holmes; *The Hound of the Baskervilles*)

*This girl had been devoted to him. A man always finds it hard to realize that he may have finally lost a woman's love, however badly he may have treated her.* (Holmes; *The Musgrave Ritual*)

*The pressure of public opinion can do in the town what the law cannot accomplish.* (Holmes; *The Copper Beeches*)

*There are some trees, Watson, which grow to a certain height, and then suddenly develop some unsightly eccentricity. You will see it often in humans.* (Holmes; *The Empty House*)

**Ask: What is in their interest to do?**
*He had a motive in misleading us.* (Holmes; *The Devil's Foot*)

*Well, yes, of course the pay is good--too good. That is what makes me uneasy. Why should they give you £120 a year, when they could have their pick for £40? There must be some strong reason behind.* (Holmes; *The Adventure of the Copper Beeches*)

*I am afraid Joseph's character is a rather deeper and more dangerous one than one might judge from his appearance. From what I have heard from him this morning, I gather that he has lost heavily in dabbling with stocks, and that he is ready to do anything on earth to better his fortunes.* (Holmes; *The Naval Treaty*)

*The exclusion from his clubs would mean ruin to Moran, who lived by his ill-gotten card-gains. He therefore murdered Adair, who at the time was endeavouring to work out how much money he should himself return, since he could not profit by his partner's foul play.* (Holmes; *The Empty House*)

*It was equally clear that the only man who really profited by the incident, as far as we could see, was the stepfather.* (Holmes; *A Case of Identity*)

*He remarks that, while the individual man is an insoluble puzzle, in the aggregate he becomes a mathematical certainty. You can, for example, never foretell what any one man will do, but you can say with precision what an average number will be up to. Individuals vary, but percentages remain constant. So says the statistician.* (Holmes; *The Sign of the Four*)

**But knowledge doesn't automatically make us wise – the most learned are not the wisest**
*Judgment can do without knowledge but not knowledge without judgment.* (Montaigne)

**Don't forget common sense**
*My simple art...is but systematized common sense.*
(Holmes; The Blanched Soldier)

**Sorrow is often wisdom's companion but it is better to learn from others sorrow to prevent our own**
*Should they in the future join their forces, as seems not unlikely, the financial world may find that Mr. Neil Gibson has learned something in that schoolroom of sorrow where our earthly lessons are taught.* (Holmes; Thor Bridge)

**Practice is a good instructor and teaches us to where to look and what to look for**
*Before turning to those moral and mental aspects of the matter which present the greatest difficulties, let the inquirer begin by mastering more elementary problems. Let him on meeting a fellow-mortal, learn at a glance to distinguish the history of the man and the trade or profession to which he belongs. Puerile as such an exercise may seem, it sharpens the faculties of observation, and teaches one where to look and what to look for.* (Holmes; A Study in Scarlet)

**And learning never stops**
*"But what I can't make head or tail of, Mr. Holmes, is how on earth you got yourself mixed up in the matter."
"Education, Gregson, education. Still seeking knowledge at the old university."* (Holmes; The Red Circle)

*Like all other arts, the Science of Deduction and Analysis is one which can only be acquired by long and patient study, nor is life long enough to allow any mortal to attain the highest possible perfection in it.* (Holmes; *A Study in Scarlet*)

*Education never ends, Watson. It is a series of lessons with the greatest for the last.* (Holmes; *The Red Circle*)

## ON SOLVING A CASE – Observation and Inference

*Cultivate absolute accuracy in observation, and truthfulness in report.* (Joseph Bell; *Dr Joe Bell*)

*It does certainly look like a hopeless case...and I see no way out of it at present. But I make it a rule, in all cases, to proceed on the strictly classical lines of inductive inquiry--collect facts, make hypotheses, test them and seek for verification. And I always endeavour to keep a perfectly open mind.* (Dr. Thorndyke; *The Red Thumb Mark*)

*It is very evident that in this we have two main processes to bear in mind and keep strictly distinct, first, the collection of the observations, and second, the inferences to be drawn from them.* (Thomas McCrae; *The Method of Zadig*)

*Keeping these separate is essential to any orderly solution of our daily problems, but how difficult this is for the majority of us is brought home to every teacher. Take a group of students who are working at physical diagnosis and it is a constant struggle to keep them making observations and not giving inferences-usually from insufficient observations, if from any at all.* (Thomas McCrae; *The Method of Zadig*)

*Observation is a matter of patience, training and thoroughness, in all of which a man may improve himself, but the use which he makes of his observations is partly a matter of his mental equipment. True he can train his powers of thought and judgment to some extent, but, we vary greatly in the quality of our*

16

*cerebral cells, and the saying of the father of medicine, "Experience is fallacious and judgment difficult," is always true. To observe correctly and decide wrongly is sure to happen to the best of us, but to observe carelessly happens only when we permit it.* (Thomas McCrae; *The Method of Zadig*)

## What is the problem? What do we ultimately want to achieve or avoid?
*That is the problem which we have to solve.* (Holmes; *The Cardboard Box*)

*Sherlock Holmes's smallest actions were all directed towards some definite and practical end.* (Dr. Watson; *A Study in Scarlet*)

## Diseases must be diagnosed before they can be cured. And if the diagnosis is wrong, the prescription will be wrong
*It is not to be imagined that he should know the remedies of diseases who knows not their original causes.* (A.C. Celsus)

## See Things for What They Are
*Do you remember the fine saying of Bossuet? "The greatest sign of an ill-regulated mind is to believe things because you wish them to be so."* (Louis Pasteur)

## Never jump to conclusions and try to collect facts as open-minded as possible
*No one can give rules for methods of thinking but it is possible to carry certain principles into operation. One is to strive to be delivered from hasty judgments. "Men see a little, presume a good deal, and so jump to the*

conclusion." *How common this is needs only a little study of our mental processes. In some this is a habit, in others a fault of education.* (Thomas McCrae; *The Method of Zadig*)

*"Shall I go for the police?"*
*"We must define the situation a little more clearly. It may bear some more innocent interpretation."*
(Holmes; *The Red Circle*)

*We approached the case...with an absolutely blank mind, which is always an advantage. We had formed no theories. We were there simply to observe and to draw inferences from our observations.* (Holmes; *The Cardboard Box*)

*I have not all my facts yet, but I do not think there are any insuperable difficulties. Still, it is an error to argue in front of your data. You find yourself insensibly twisting them round to fit your theories.* (Holmes; *Wisteria Lodge*)

*It is a capital mistake to theorize before one has data. Insensibly one begins to twist facts to suit theories, instead of theories to suit facts.* (Holmes; *A Scandal in Bohemia*)

*The fatal mistake which the ordinary policeman make is this, that he gets his theory first, and then makes the facts fit it, instead of getting his facts first and making all his little observations and deductions until he is driven irresistibly by them into an elucidation in a direction he may never have originally contemplated.* (Joseph Bell; *Dr. Joe Bell*)

*The point is a simple one, but the Inspector had overlooked it because he had started with the supposition that these county magnates had had nothing to do with the matter. Now, I make a point of never having any prejudices, and of following docilely wherever fact may lead me.* (Holmes; *The Reigate Squire*)

*I will not bias your mind by suggesting theories or suspicions, Watson. I wish you simply to report facts in the fullest manner to me, and you can leave me to do the theorizing.* (Holmes; *The Hound of the Baskervilles*)

## Beware of first impressions – appearances can be deceiving

*"Surely," said I, "the man's appearance would go far with any jury?"*
*"That is a dangerous argument, my dear Watson. You remember that terrible murderer, Bert Stevens, who wanted us to get him off in '87? Was there ever a more mild-mannered, Sunday-school young man?"* (Holmes; *The Norwood Builder*)

*"What a very attractive women!" I exclaimed, turning to my companion.*
*"It is of the first importance...not to allow your judgment to be biased by personal qualities...The emotional qualities are antagonistic to clear reasoning. I assure you that the most winning woman I ever knew was hanged for poisoning three little children for their insurance-money, and the most repellant man of my acquaintance is a philanthropist who has spent nearly a quarter of a million upon the London poor."* (Holmes; *The Sign of the Four*)

*Dear me! Dear me!...Well, now, who would have thought it? And how deceptive appearances may be, to be sure! Such a nice young man to look at! It is a lesson to us not to trust our own judgment, is it not, Lestrade?* (Holmes; *The Norwood Builder*)

## Being nice is hardly the evidence of innocence
*Dismiss from your mind the idea that anything which the maid or her mistress may have said must necessarily be true. The lady's charming personality must not be permitted to warp our judgment.* (Holmes; *The Abbey Grange*)

## Does it make logically sense?
*"They have been identified as her clothes, and it seemed to me that if the clothes were there the body would not be far off."* (Inspector Lestrade)
*"By the same brilliant reasoning, every man's body is to be found in the neighbourhood of his wardrobe. And pray what did you hope to arrive at through this?"* (Holmes; *The Noble Bachelor*)

**OBSERVATION – Start with collecting facts and follow them where they lead**
*Observation with me is second nature.* (Holmes; *A Study in Scarlet*)

*More is missed by not looking than not knowing.* (Thomas McCrae; Medical School Axiom)

*For one mistake made for not knowing, ten mistakes are made for not looking.* (James Alexander Lindsay)

**Don't be too quick**
*Let us know a little more before we act.* (Holmes; *The Abbey Grange*)

*It is evident that if the first stage – the collection of the facts – is improperly done, we have not the basis for the second and it is bound to be wrong. The game is hopelessly lost from the start. How important, therefore, to give every effort to the collection of our facts.* (Thomas McCrae; *The Method of Zadig*)

**And don't blindly collect endless amounts of facts**
*Our steps must be guided by a clue.* (Francis Bacon)

**We can't observe or collect facts without some kind of view – what to look for, how to look and how to interpret what we see**
The professor and philosopher Karl Popper (1902 – 1994) often started his lectures by telling his audience: *"Observe!"* But we can't – we need to know *"Observe what?"* We can't observe without an idea of what we are

looking for. But we should try to gather facts as open-minded and unbiased as possible.

**Without an idea of how reality works, a purpose, provisional idea of what is important and what to look for, our observation or collection of facts is of little use**

*A hypothesis is...the obligatory starting point of all experimental reasoning. Without it no investigation would be possible, and one would learn nothing: one could only pile up barren observations. To experiment without a preconceived idea is to wonder aimlessly.* (Claude Bernard)

*How profoundly ignorant B. must be of the very soul of observation!* [B. said that Darwin should have published facts alone]. *About thirty years ago there was much talk that geologists ought only to observe and not theorise; and I well remember someone saying that at this rate a man might as well go into a gravel-pit and count the pebbles and describe the colours. How odd it is that anyone should not see that all observation must be for or against some view if it is to be of any service!* (Charles Darwin)

*"You have a theory?"*
*"Yes, a provisional one."* (Holmes; *The Yellow Face*)

*One forms provisional theories and waits for time or fuller knowledge to explore them.* (Holmes; *The Sussex Vampire*)

*"We are coming now rather into the region of guesswork,"* said Dr. Mortimer.

23

*"Say, rather, into the region where we balance probabilities and choose the most likely. It is the scientific use of the imagination, but we have always some material basis on which to start our speculation."* (Holmes; *The Hound of the Baskervilles*)

*I have already said that he must have gone to King's Pyland or to Mapleton. He is not at King's Pyland. Therefore he is at Mapleton. Let us take that as a working hypothesis and see what it leads us to.* (Holmes; *Silver Blaze*)

*Well, we can adopt it as a working hypothesis and then see how far our difficulties disappear.* (Holmes; *The Valley of Fear*)

*Nothing can be done without preconceived ideas; only there must be the wisdom not to accept their deductions beyond what experiments confirm.* (Louis Pasteur)

**What are the facts? Holmes first gathered enough evidence – both positive and negative – that was relevant to his problem**
*Data! Data! Data!...I can't make bricks without clay.* (Holmes; *The Copper Beeches*)

*I should like a few more facts before I get so far as a theory.* (Holmes; *The Valley of Fear*)

*Pray give us the essential facts from the commencement, and I can afterwards question you as to those details which seem to me to be most important.* (Holmes; *The Five Orange Pips*)

*"What do you wish me to do?"*
*"To give me a true account of all that happened at the Abbey Grange last night—a TRUE account, mind you, with nothing added and nothing taken off."* (Holmes; *The Abbey Grange*)

*I am glad of all details...whether they seem to you to be relevant or not.* (Holmes; *The Copper Beeches*)

*The temptation to form premature theories upon insufficient data is the bane of our profession.* (Holmes; *The Valley of Fear*)

*I had...come to an entirely erroneous conclusion which shows, my dear Watson, how dangerous it always is to reason from insufficient data.* (Holmes; *The Speckled Band*)

*"You're like a surgeon who wants every symptom before he can give his diagnosis."*
*"Exactly. That expresses it."* (Holmes; *Thor Bridge*)

*It is usually wiser to tell the truth.* (Holmes; *The Veiled Lodger*)

*The principal difference between a good and a bad diagnostician is usually a matter of thoroughness and method. Brains count, of course, but the man who has not collected his facts has but little chance to use his brains.* (Thomas McCrae; *The Method of Zadig*)

**Make sure "facts" are facts – Is it really so? Is this really true? Did this really happen?**
*I realize that if you ask people to account for "facts", they usually spend more time finding reasons for them than finding out whether they are true...They skip over the facts but carefully deduce inferences. They normally begin thus: "How does this come about?" But does it do so? That is what they ought to be asking.* (Montaigne)

*This case is quite sufficiently complicated to start with without the further difficulty of false information.* (Holmes; *Thor Bridge*)

**Deception has many faces**
*I had never known him to be wrong and yet the keenest reasoner may occasionally be deceived.* (Dr. Watson; *The Valley of Fear*)

*If falsehood, like truth, had only one face, we would be in better shape. For we would take as certain the opposite of what the liar said. But the reverse of truth has a hundred thousand shapes and a limitless field.* (Montaigne)

*His soft, precise fashion of speech leaves a conviction of sincerity which a mere bully could not produce.* (Holmes; *The Final Problem*)

*It is only a patient who has an object in deceiving his surgeon who would conceal the facts of his case.* (Holmes; *Thor Bridge*)

*Observe that rule laid down by Chilo, Nothing to excess...Not to believe too rashly: not to disbelieve too easily.* (Montaigne)

## Why may they be lying or deceive us? What is out of the ordinary?

*Why are they lying, and what is the truth which they are trying so hard to conceal? Let us try, Watson, you and I, if we can get behind the lie and reconstruct the truth.* (Holmes; The Valley of Fear)

*How do I know that they are lying? Because it is a clumsy fabrication which simply could not be true. Consider! According to the story given to us, the assassin had less than a minute after the murder had been committed to take that ring, which was under another ring, from the dead man's finger, to replace the other ring - a thing which he would surely never have done - and to put that singular card beside his victim. I say that this was obviously impossible.* (Holmes; The Valley of Fear)

*"But have you told me all?"* (Holmes)
*"Yes, all."*
*"Miss Roylott, you have not. You are screening your stepfather."*
*"Why, what do you mean?*
*For answer Holmes pushed back the frill of black lace which fringed the hand that lay upon our visitor's knee. Five little livid spots, the marks of four fingers and a thumb, were printed upon the white wrist.*
*"You have been cruelly used."* (The Speckled Band)

*All the time that she was telling me this story she never
once looked in my direction, and her voice was quite
unlike her usual tones. It was evident to me that she
was saying what was false. I said nothing in reply, but
turned my face to the wall, sick at heart, with my mind
filled with a thousand venomous doubts and suspicions.
What was it that my wife was concealing from me?*
(Grant Munro – character in *The Yellow Face*)

*We must look for consistency. Where there is a want of
it we must suspect deception.* (Holmes; *Thor Bridge*)

## Don't miss the forest for the trees – It is not the amount of information that counts but the relevant one.

*The principal difficulty in your case...lay in the fact of
there being too much evidence. What was vital was
overlaid and hidden by what was irrelevant. Of all the
facts which were presented to us we had to pick just
those which we deemed to be essential, and then piece
them together in their order, so as to reconstruct this
very remarkable chain of events.* (Holmes; *The Naval
Treaty*)

## Separate the relevant and important facts from the unimportant or accidental

*The first thing was to look at the facts and separate
what was certain from what was conjecture.* (A.C.
Doyle, *Memories and Adventures*)

*It is of the highest importance in the art of detection to
be able to recognize out of a number of facts which are
incidental and which are vital. Otherwise your energy*

*and attention must be dissipated instead of being concentrated.* (Holmes; *The Reigate Squire*)

*One cannot always have the success for which one hopes. An investigator needs facts and not legends or rumours.* (Holmes; *The Hound of the Baskervilles*)

*Having gathered these facts, Watson, I smoked several pipes over them, trying to separate those which were crucial from others which were merely incidental.* (Holmes; *The Crooked Man*)

*Before we start to investigate that, let us try to realize what we do know, so as to make the most of it, and to separate the essential from the accidental.* (Holmes; *The Priory School*)

*It is one of those cases where the art of the reasoner should be used rather for the sifting of details than for the acquiring of fresh evidence. The tragedy has been so uncommon, so complete and of such personal importance to so many people, that we are suffering from a plethora of surmise, conjecture, and hypothesis. The difficulty is to detach the framework of fact--of absolute undeniable fact--from the embellishments of theorists and reporters. Then, having established ourselves upon this sound basis, it is our duty to see what inferences may be drawn and what are the special points upon which the whole mystery turns.* (Holmes; *Silver Blaze*)

*Though most of the facts were familiar to me, I had not sufficiently appreciated their relative importance, nor their connection to each other.* (Holmes; *Silver Blaze*)

**There may be many theories that fit the facts**
*There should be no combination of events for which the wit of man cannot conceive an explanation.* (Holmes; *The Valley of Fear*)

*Circumstantial evidence is occasionally very convincing, as when you find a trout in the milk.* (Holmes; *The Noble Bachelor*)

*Circumstantial evidence is a very tricky thing...It may seem to point very straight to one thing, but if you shift your own point of view a little, you may find it pointing in an equally uncompromising manner to something entirely different.* (Holmes; *The Boscombe Valley Mystery*)

**Sometimes it helps to shift perspective**
*No, no. No crime...Only one of those whimsical little incidents which will happen when you have four million human beings all jostling each other within the space of a few square miles. Amid the action and reaction of so dense a swarm of humanity, every possible combination of events may be expected to take place, and many a little problem will be presented which may be striking and bizarre without being criminal.* (Holmes; *The Blue Carbuncle*)

**More information isn't necessarily better information but it may falsely increase our confidence – What is not worth knowing is not worth knowing**
*A wise man sees as much as he ought, not as much as he can.* (Montaigne)

**Get down to the roots of the matter**
*Some facts should be suppressed, or at least a just sense
of proportion should be observed in treating them.*
(Holmes; *The Sign of the Four*)

*I fear, sir...that, interesting and indeed essential as
these details are, my inquiries must go more to the root
of things.* (Holmes; *The Second Stain*)

*"But what is at the root of it?"*
*"Ah, yes, Watson -- severely practical, as usual! What is
at the root of it all."* (Holmes; *The Red Circle*)

**Know where to look**
*"You appeared to read a good deal upon her which was
quite invisible to me," I remarked.*
*"Not invisible but unnoticed, Watson. You did not know
where to look, and so you missed all that was
important."* (Holmes; *A Case of Identity*)

*Yes indeed you see, we all see, but often you do not
observe.* (Joseph Bell, *Dr. Joe Bell*)

*"You see, but you do not observe. The distinction is
clear. For example, you have frequently seen the steps
which lead up from the hall to this room."* (Holmes)
*"Frequently."*
*"How often?"*
*"Well, some hundreds of times."*
*"Then how many are there?"*
*"How many! I don't know."*
*"Quite so! You have not observed. And yet you have
seen. That is just my point. Now, I know that there are*

31

*seventeen steps, because I have both seen and observed." (A Scandal in Bohemia)*

*This was overlooked because it was in the darkest corner of the room, and no one thought of looking there.* (Inspector Lestrade – a fictional Scotland Yard detective; *A Study in Scarlet*)

*It was invisible, buried in the mud. I only saw it because I was looking for it.* (Holmes; *Silver Blaze*)

*"By George!" cried the inspector. "How ever did you see that?"*
*"Because I looked for it."* (Holmes; *The Dancing Men*)

*The world is full of obvious things which nobody by any chance ever observes.* (Holmes; *The Hound of the Baskervilles*)

*"You speak of danger. You have evidently seen more in these rooms than was visible to me."*
*"No, but I fancy that I may have deduced a little more. I imagine that you saw all that I did."* (Holmes; *The Speckled Band*)

*"I can see nothing," said I, handing it back to my friend. "On the contrary, Watson, you can see everything. You fail, however, to reason from what you see. You are too timid in drawing your inferences."* (Holmes; *The Blue Carbuncle*)

## The eye sees only what it is trained to see
*In the last analysis, we see only what we are ready to see, what we have been taught to see. We eliminate and*

*ignore everything that is not a part of our prejudices.*
(Jean-Martin Charcot)

*The necessary knowledge is that of what to observe.* (C.
Auguste Dupin, *The Murders in the Rue Morgue*)

*The value of experience is not in seeing much, but in
seeing wisely.* (William Osler)

*I see no more than you, but I have trained myself to
notice what I see.* (Holmes; *The Blanched Soldier*)

*Perhaps I have trained myself to see what others
overlook.* (Holmes; *A Case of Identity*)

*Louis* [Pierre Charles Alexandre Louis] *introduced what
is known as the Numerical Method, a plan which we
use every day, though the phrase is not now very often
on our lips. The guiding motto of his life was
"Arsmedicatota in observationibus", in carefully
observing facts, carefully collating them, carefully
analysing them. To get an accurate knowledge of any
disease it is necessary to study a large series of cases
and to go into all the particulars – the conditions under
which it is met, the subjects specially liable, the various
symptoms, the pathological changes, the effects of
drugs. This method, so simple, so self-evident, we owe
largely to Louis.* (William Osler)

*How can a man train his powers of observation? By
use, may be answered, but this is not everything. Use
may be careless and lead to deterioration rather than
to improvement. It must be a use which involves proper
method and thoroughness. For some of us the training*

which was given to Kim in Kipling's story of that name *may be helpful. He was trained for work in the secret service in India and at one stage under Lurgan Sahib he was allowed to look for a minute at a tray which contained various objects. It was then covered and he was required to detail what was on the tray. To Kim's enquiry as to how another had attained greater accuracy than himself in doing this, the answer was, "By doing it many times over till it is done perfectly-for it is worth doing." We might all carry this around as a daily reminder.* (Thomas McCrae; *The Method of Zadig*)

*But nothing which trains the powers of observation can be unimportant, and far from being tiresome it adds to the interest of the day. "Strive to be one of those upon whom nothing is lost," said a wise teacher.* (Thomas McCrae; *The Method of Zadig*)

**"Checklist" routines for critical factors help – assuming I am competent enough to decide what factors are critical and that I can evaluate them**
*The student or practitioner has to keep himself to the routine of noting point after point in its order and not to be tempted to look into some interesting condition first.* (Thomas McCrae; *The Method of Zadig*)

*The acquirement of method is more or less possible for us all...It is only by adhering rigidly to a definite routine with patient after patient and day after day that a proper reflex can be obtained.* (Thomas McCrae; *The Method of Zadig*)

*In the beginning one has to determine that every point is going to be investigated in regular order, and it is important that this order should be invariable, for if one switches about from one routine to another many things will be missed.* (Thomas McCrae; *The Method of Zadig*)

*To practise order and system requires steady adherence to a given plan until the order of events becomes unconscious. With training one observation follows another without any effort and a glance will do what formerly took repeated observations.* (Thomas McCrae; *The Method of Zadig*)

## What seems like a small thing may be of great significance
*The smallest point may be the most essential.* (Holmes; *The Red Circle*)

*All this seems strange to you...because you failed at the beginning of the inquiry to grasp the importance of the single real clue which was presented to you.* (Holmes; *A Study in Scarlet*)

## We need to both observe the big picture – forest – and the details – trees – Sometimes the trivial or the most immaterial aspect of a case may be the most important but we need to learn how to separate between trifles that matter and those that don't
*"You have an extraordinary genius for minutiae," I remarked.*
*"I appreciate their importance."* (Holmes; *The Sign of the Four*)

*It has long been an axiom of mine that the little things are infinitely the most important.* (Holmes; *A Case of Identity*)

*You know my method. It is founded upon the observation of trifles.* (Holmes; *The Boscombe Valley Mystery*)

*What seems strange to you is only so because you do not follow my train of thought or observe the small facts upon which large inferences may depend.* (Holmes; *The Sign of the Four*)

*I always impressed over and over again upon all my scholars – Conan Doyle among them – the vast importance of little distinctions, the endless significance of trifles.* (Joseph Bell; *Joseph Bell: An Appreciation by an Old Friend*)

*It is just these very simple things which are extremely liable to be overlooked.* (Holmes; *The Sign of the Four*)

*Never trust to general impressions, my boy, but concentrate yourself upon details.* (Holmes; *A Case of Identity*)

*You never learn that the gravest issues may depend upon the smallest things.* (Holmes; *The Creeping Man*)

*The great majority of people, of incidents, and of cases resemble each other in the main and larger features...Most men have...a head, two arms, a nose, a mouth, and a certain number of teeth. It is the little differences, themselves trifles, such as the droop of an eyelid, or what not, which differentiates man.* (Joseph Bell; *Dr. Joe Bell*)

## What have we overlooked?
*It is one of those instances where the reasoned can produce an effect which seems remarkable to his neighbour, because the latter has missed the one little point which is the basis of the deduction.* (Holmes; *The Crooked Man*)

## Sometimes we overlook that which is most obvious
*In searching for the obscure, do not overlook the obvious.* (James Alexander Lindsay)

**What we see is all we think is there– What often leads us astray in an investigation is that we adopt the theory which is most likely to account for the "visible" and found facts but what if the important is left out? What is not reported, withheld, hidden?**

**If we don't see this evidence, why not? Is it not normally possible to see? Is it being hidden from us – deliberate or not? Can't it be seen? Or have we not actively looked for it?**

## Sometimes luck comes our way
*"Mr. Holmes…I do not know how to express my gratitude. Even now I do not understand how you attained this result."*
*"Simply by having the good fortune to get the right clue from the beginning."* (Holmes; *Black Peter*)

*"Then how in the name of all that is wonderful did you get these facts? They are absolutely correct in every particular."*

*"Ah, that is good luck. I could only say what was the balance of probability. I did not at all expect to be so accurate."* (Holmes; *The Sign of the Four*)

## DEDUCTION – What inferences can we draw from our observations and facts?

*All day I turned these facts over in my mind, endeavouring to hit upon some theory which could reconcile them all, and to find that line of least resistance which my poor friend had declared to be the starting-point of every investigation.* (Dr. Watson; *The Final Problem*)

*But we hold several threads in our hands, and the odds are that one or other of them guides us to the truth. We may waste time in following the wrong one, but sooner or later we must come upon the right.* (Holmes; *The Hound of the Baskervilles*)

## Reasoning backwards – working back from observations/effects to causes

*The essential factor in this method consists in working back from observations of conditions to the causes which brought them about. It is often a question of deciding the doings of yesterday by the records found to-day.* (Thomas McCrae; *The Method of Zadig*)

*The ideal reasoner...would, when he had once been shown a single fact in all its bearings, deduce from it not only all the chain of events which led up to it but also all the results which would follow from it.* (Holmes; *The Five Orange Pips*)

*The only point in the case which deserved mention was the curious analytical reasoning from effects to causes, by which I succeeded in unraveling it.* (Holmes; *The Sign of the Four*)

*In solving a problem of this sort, the grand thing is to be able to reason backward. That is a very useful accomplishment, and a very easy one, but people do not practice it much. In the everyday affairs of life it is more useful to reason forward, and so the other comes to be neglected.* (Holmes; *A Study in Scarlet*)

*Most people, if you describe a train of events to them, will tell you what the result would be. They can put those events together in their minds, and argue from them that something will come to pass. There are few people, however, who, if you told them a result, would be able to evolve from their own inner consciousness what the steps were which led up to that result. This power is what I mean when I talk of reasoning backward, or analytically.* (Holmes; *A Study in Scarlet*)

## Use the simplest means first
*Now we must set ourselves very seriously to finding this gentleman and ascertaining what part he has played in this little mystery. To do this, we must try the simplest means first, and these lie undoubtedly in an advertisement in all the evening papers. If this fail, I shall have recourse to other methods.* (Holmes; *The Blue Carbuncle*)

## Sometimes things are not as simple as they seem. But sometimes they are not as complex as they seem, either
*Surely it is no great feat to assume that a man who treats a fifty-guinea watch so cavalierly must be a careless man. Neither is it a very far fetched inference that a man who inherits one article of such value is*

*pretty well provided for in other respects.* (Holmes; *The Sign of the Four*)

## Sometimes the solution is simple
*Perhaps, when a man has special knowledge and special powers like my own, it rather encourages him to seek a complex explanation when a simpler one is at hand.* (Holmes; *The Adventure of the Abbey Grange*)

*The case has been an interesting one...because it serves to show very clearly how simple the explanation may be of an affair which at first sight seems to be almost inexplicable.* (Holmes; *The Noble Bachelor*)

## Which is the simplest, most natural explanation – the one requiring the least assumptions needed to explain the facts?
*There never was a sounder logical maxim of scientific procedure than Ockham's razor...before you try a complicated hypothesis, you should make quite sure that no simplification of it will explain the facts equally well.* (Charles Sanders Peirce)

*I was already firmly convinced, Watson, that there were not three separate mysteries here, but one.* (Holmes; *The Musgrave Ritual*)

## But don't try to over-simplify complex matters – especially when we deal with systems with complicated interactions
*It is rarely permissible to base a diagnosis upon a single sign.* (James Alexander Lindsay)

*The inferences to be drawn from the observations—is a very different matter. Here the possibilities of error are much greater and what seems a simple diagnosis may involve complex inferences. A frequent mistake is to fail to recognize that there is any question of inference and to think that physical signs give a diagnosis directly.* (Thomas McCrae; *The Method of Zadig*)

*All parts of a living body are interrelated; they can act only in so far as they act all together; trying to separate one from the whole means transferring it to the realm of dead substances. It means entirely changing its essence.* (Georges Cuvier)

**What normally happens in similar situations? Why should this be any different?**
*When you hear hoof beats behind you, don't expect to see a zebra.* (Proverb)

*Think of common diseases first..."Queer cases" are usually abnormal types of common conditions.* (James Alexander Lindsay)

*Common diseases cause uncommon symptoms more often than uncommon diseases cause common symptoms.* (Medical maxim)

*Sometimes we are saved from error by our lack of knowledge of the finer points of the game. I well remember a fellow house-officer and myself being much interested in the diagnosis of an obscure abdominal condition. We went over it from every side and to the best of our ability, coming at last to a diagnosis. The attending physician was much* interested and examined the patient very carefully, at last making a diagnosis which had never even occurred to us to consider. He suggested a rare condition which neither of us had ever seen but we felt that consideration of it should not have escaped us. We were in a very humble frame of mind until the operation showed that our diagnosis had been right. It was so principally because the rare condition had not come to our minds. The moral of this is not that ignorance is an advantage. But some of us are too much attracted by the thought of rare things and forget the law of averages in diagnosis. There is a man who is very proud of having diagnosed a rare abdominal disease on several occasions. But as for some years he made this diagnosis in every obscure abdominal condition, of course being nearly always wrong one cannot feel that he deserves much credit. (Thomas McCrae; *The Method of Zadig*)

As you are aware E is the most common letter in the English alphabet and it predominates to so marked an extent that even in a short sentence one would expect to find it most often. Out of fifteen symbols in the first message four were the same, so it was reasonable to set this down as E. (Holmes; *The Dancing Men*)

**History often repeats itself**
There is nothing new under the sun. It has all been done before. (Holmes; *A Study in Scarlet*)

Mr. Mac, the most practical thing that you ever did in your life would be to shut yourself up for three months and read twelve hours a day at the annals of crime. Everything comes in circles...The old wheel turns, and the same spoke comes up. It's all been done before, and will be again. (Holmes; *The Valley of Fear*)

**Analogies – What does this case resemble? What is the same between this situation and others?**

**Holmes often sees a link to a situation he have seen before and he have a rich repertoire of more general knowledge that can be used in a variety of occasions**
*They lay all the evidence before me, and I am generally able, by the help of my knowledge of the history of crime, to set them straight. There is a strong family resemblance about misdeeds, and if you have all the details of a thousand at your finger ends, it is odd if you can't unravel the thousand and first.* (Holmes; *A Study in Scarlet*)

*"But I have heard all that you have heard."*
*"Without, however, the knowledge of pre-existing cases which serves me so well. There was a parallel instance in Aberdeen some years back, and something on very much the same lines at Munich the year after the Franco-Prussian War."* (Holmes; *The Noble Bachelor*)

*It reminds me of the circumstances attendant on the death of Van Jansen, in Utrecht, in the year "34."* (Holmes; *A Study in Scarlet*)

*You will find parallel cases, if you consult my index, in Andover in '77, and there was something of the sort at The Hague last year.* (Holmes; *A Case of Identity*)

*The case was concerned with a will and possessed some features of interest. I was able to refer him to two parallel cases, the one at Riga in 1857, and the other at St. Louis in 1871, which have suggested to him the true solution.* (Holmes; *The Sign of the Four*)

*Whimsical and bizarre conceits of this kind are common enough in the annals of crime and usually afford valuable indications as to the criminal.* (Holmes; *The Sign of the Four*)

*All knowledge comes useful to the detective...Even the trivial fact that in the year 1865 a picture by Greuze entitled La JeuneFille a l'Agneau fetched one million two hundred thousand francs—more than forty thousand pounds—at the Portalis sale may start a train of reflection in your mind.* (Holmes; *The Valley of Fear*)

*I fancy that among your extensive archives, Watson, you may find some which were nearly as obscure.* (Holmes; *The Devils's Foot*)

*I am an omnivorous reader with a strangely retentive memory for trifles. That phrase "the Lion's Mane" haunted my mind. I knew that I had seen it somewhere in an unexpected context.* (Holmes; *The Lion's Mane*)

**But sometimes we learn more by looking for differences – not similarities – in situations**
*In teaching the treatment of disease and accident, all careful teachers have first to show the student how to recognize accurately the case. The recognition depends in great measure on the accurate and rapid appreciation of small points in which the diseased*

*differs from the health state. In fact, the student must be taught first to observe carefully.* (Joseph Bell; *Dr. Joe Bell*)

**Patterns repeat but not always – Is it the same situation or circumstances or is it unique and fundamentally different from the past – what factors, conditions, behavior differ? Was it a random factor?**
*We ought not to be ignorant that the same remedies are not good for all.* (Celsus)

**But remember that we see what we are looking for – if we look for similarities, this is what we see, if we look for the differences, that is what we find.**

**Paradoxically the strange crime is often easier to solve than the common one**
*I have already explained to you that what is out of the common is usually a guide rather than a hindrance.* (Holmes; *A Study in Scarlet*)

*It is only the colourless, uneventful case which is hopeless.* (Holmes; *Shoscombe Old Place*)

*"It seems, from what I gather, to be one of those simple cases which are so extremely difficult."*
*"That sounds a little paradoxical."*
*"But it is profoundly true. Singularity is almost invariably a clue. The more featureless and commonplace a crime is, the more difficult it is to bring it home."* (Holmes; *The Boscombe Valley Mystery*)

*The most difficult crime to track is the one which is purposeless. Now this is not purposeless. Who is it who profits by it?* (Holmes; *The Naval Treaty*)

*As a rule...the more bizarre a thing is the less mysterious it proves to be. It is your commonplace, featureless crimes which are really puzzling, just as a commonplace face is the most difficult to identify.* (Holmes; *The Red-Headed League*)

*It is a mistake to confound strangeness with mystery. The most commonplace crime is often the most mysterious, because it presents no new or special features from which deductions may be drawn. This murder would have been infinitely more difficult to unravel had the body of the victim been simply found lying in the roadway without any of those outré and sensational accompaniments which have rendered it remarkable. These strange details, far from making the case more difficult, have really had the effect of making it less so.* (Holmes; *A Study in Scarlet*)

*The larger crimes are apt to be the simpler, for the bigger the crime the more obvious, as a rule, is the motive.* (Holmes; *A Case of Identity*)

**But not always**
*You have heard me remark that the strangest and most unique things are very often connected not with the larger but with the smaller crimes, and occasionally, indeed, where there is room for doubt whether any positive crime has been committed...As a rule, when I have heard some slight indication of the course of events, I am able to guide myself by the thousands of*

*other similar cases which occur to my memory. In the present instance I am forced to admit that the facts are, to the best of my belief, unique.* (Holmes; *The Red-Headed League*)

*The more outré and grotesque an incident is the more carefully it deserves to be examined, and the very point which appears to complicate a case is, when duly considered and scientifically handled, the one which is most likely to elucidate it.* (Holmes; *The Hound of the Baskervilles*)

*It appears to me that this mystery in considered insoluble, for the very reason which should cause it to be regarded as easy of solution – I mean for the outré character of its features...In investigations such as we are now pursuing, it should not be so much asked "what has occurred," as "what has occurred that has never occurred before."* (C. Auguste Dupin, *The Murders in the Rue Morgue*)

*Students of criminology will remember the analogous incidents in Godno, in Little Russia, in the year '66, and of course there are the Anderson murders in North Carolina, but this case possesses some features which are entirely its own.* (Holmes; *The Hound of the Baskervilles*)

*I think anything out of the ordinary routine of life well worth reporting.* (Holmes; *The Hound of the Baskervilles*)

**When an event differs from what Holmes expect, it draws his attention – What is out of the ordinary or atypical?**

**The absence of something we expect to see or happen is information and a clue in itself**
*"Is there any point to which you would wish to draw my attention?"*
*"To the curious incident of the dog in the night-time."*
*"The dog did nothing in the night-time."*
*"That was the curious incident," remarked Sherlock Holmes. (Silver Blaze)*

**Holmes expected the relationship to be dog: stranger→ Barking. But he observed that the dog didn't bark. And if the dog didn't bark it must be because the dog knew the midnight visitor. Then the relationship must have been dog: familiar person**
*I had grasped the significance of the silence of the dog, for one true inference invariably suggests others...a dog was kept in the stables, and yet, though some one had been in and had fetched out a horse, he had not barked enough to arouse the two lads in the loft. Obviously the midnight visitor was some one whom the dog knew well. (Holmes; Silver Blaze)*

**Negative evidence and events that don't happen, matter when something implies they should be present or happen**
*Only one important thing has happened in the last three days, and that is that nothing has happened. (Holmes; The Second Stain)*

*When I came to examine the address of the packet I observed that it was to Miss S. Cushing. Now, the oldest sister would, of course, be Miss Cushing, and although her initial was "S" it might belong to one of the others as well. In that case we should have to commence our investigation from a fresh basis altogether. I therefore went into the house with the intention of clearing up this point. I was about to assure Miss Cushing that I was convinced that a mistake had been made when you may remember that I came suddenly to a stop. The fact was that I had just seen something which filled me with surprise and at the same time narrowed the field of our inquiry immensely.* (Holmes; *The Cardboard Box*)

*"You found something compromising?"*
*"Absolutely nothing. That was what amazed me. However, you have now seen the point of the picture. It shows him to be a very wealthy man. How did he acquire wealth? He is unmarried. His younger brother is a station master in the west of England. His chair is worth seven hundred a year. And he owns a Greuze."* (Holmes)
*"Well?"*
*"Surely the inference is plain."*
*"You mean that he has a great income and that he must earn it in an illegal fashion?"*
*"Exactly. Of course I have other reasons for thinking so—dozens of exiguous threads which lead vaguely up towards the centre of the web where the poisonous, motionless creature is lurking. I only mention the Greuze because it brings the matter within the range of your own observation."* (*The Valley of Fear*)

*"Dumb-bell -- there's only one. Where's the other?"*
*"I don't know, Mr. Holmes. There may have been only one. I have not noticed them for months."*
*"One dumb-bell – " Holmes said seriously...*
*"You will remember, Inspector MacDonald, that I was somewhat struck by the absence of a dumb-bell..."*
*"All my lines of thought lead me back invariably to the one basic question—why should an athletic man develop his frame upon so unnatural an instrument as a single dumb-bell?"* (Holmes; *The Valley of Fear*)

**Small pieces of information may in themselves look to be of no importance but may clarify things when taken together.**
*Let us take it link by link.* (Holmes; *Wisteria Lodge*)

*You see all these isolated facts, together with many minor ones, all pointed in the same direction.* (Holmes; *A Case of Identity*)

*Remarkable, is it not? But consider the facts. Is it a coincidence that it is found at the very point where the train pitches and sways as it comes round on the points? Is not that the place where an object upon the roof might be expected to fall off? The points would affect no object inside the train. Either the body fell from the roof, or a very curious coincidence has occurred. But now consider the question of the blood. Of course, there was no bleeding on the line if the body had bled elsewhere. Each fact is suggestive in itself. Together they have a cumulative force.* (Holmes; *The Bruce-Partington Plans*)

*Experience has shown...that a vast, perhaps the larger, portion of truth arises from the seemingly irrelevant.* (C. Auguste Dupin; *The Mystery of Marie Roget*)

*We mustn't expect too much, Jervis...in fact we have no reason to expect anything. We are just looking over this jetsam as a matter of routine to note any facts that it may seem to suggest, without regard to their apparent relevancy or irrelevancy to our inquiry. You cannot judge the relevancy of an isolated fact. Experience has taught me, and must have taught you, that the most trivial, commonplace and seemingly irrelevant facts have a way of suddenly assuming a crucial importance by connecting, explaining or filling in the detail of later discoveries.* (Dr. Thorndyke; *The Penrose Mystery*)

**Strip away things that don't count and focus on what matters – the core**

**Eliminate possibilities – What can we exclude? – Assuming the true solution or explanation is among the considered possibilities**
*Another point is to endeavour to cultivate the habit of orderly thinking exactly as of orderly examination. This should be within the power of the majority and is worth every effort. As a rule it is possible in a problem of diagnosis to state all the possibilities and by exclusion narrow them down to one, possibly to two or more.* (Thomas McCrae; *The Method of Zadig*)

*Such was the problem which my visitor laid before me. It presented, as the astute reader will have already perceived, few difficulties in its solution, for a very limited choice of alternatives must get to the root of the*

52

matter. Still, elementary as it was, there were points of interest and novelty about it which may excuse my placing it upon record. I now proceeded, using my familiar method of logical analysis, to narrow down the possible solutions. (Holmes; *The Blanched Soldier*)

"But very few books would correspond with that."
"Exactly. Therein lies our salvation. Our search is narrowed down to standardized books which anyone may be supposed to possess." (Holmes; *The Valley of Fear*)

**What doesn't matter? What can't happen? What can't it be? What can't be done?**
*It seems to me to have only one drawback, Hopkins, and that is that it is intrinsically impossible. Have you tried to drive a harpoon through a body? No? Tut, tut, my dear sir, you must really pay attention to these details.* (Holmes; *Black Peter*)

"We must look for consistency. Where there is a want of it we must suspect deception." (Holmes)
"I hardly follow you."
"Well now, Watson, suppose for a moment that we visualize you in the character of a woman who, in a cold, premeditated fashion, is about to get rid of a rival. You have planned it. A note has been written. The victim has come. You have your weapon. The crime is done. It has been workmanlike and complete. Do you tell me that after carrying out so crafty a crime you would now ruin your reputation as a criminal by forgetting to fling your weapon into those adjacent reed-beds which would forever cover it, but you must needs carry it carefully home and put it in your own

*wardrobe, the very first place that would be searched? Your best friends would hardly call you a schemer, Watson, and yet I could not picture you doing anything so crude as that."*
*"In the excitement of the moment – "*
*"No, no, Watson, I will not admit that it is possible. Where a crime is cooly premeditated, then the means of covering it are coolly premeditated also. I hope, therefore, that we are in the presence of a serious misconception." (Thor Bridge)*

*By the method of exclusion, I had arrived at this result, for no other hypothesis would meet the facts. (Holmes; A Study in Scarlet)*

*As it was first presented to me, there were three possible explanations of the seclusion or incarceration of this gentleman in an outhouse of his father's mansion. There was the explanation that he was in hiding for a crime, or that he was mad and that they wished to avoid an asylum, or that he had some disease which caused his segregation. I could think of no other adequate solutions. These, then, had to be sifted and balanced against each other. (Holmes; The Blanched Soldier)*

*What could that something be? She could not have...she could hardly have...You see we have already arrived, by a process of exclusion, at the idea that she might have seen an American. (Holmes; The Noble Bachelor)*

*"It could not have been..."*
*"So, by the process of exclusion, we arrive at the fact that he..." (Holmes; The Solitary Cyclist)*

"It's devilish, Mr. Holmes, devilish!" cried Mortimer Tregennis. "It is not of this world. Something has come into that room which has dashed the light of reason from their minds. What human contrivance could do that?"

"I fear," said Holmes, "that if the matter is beyond humanity it is certainly beyond me. Yet we must exhaust all natural explanations before we fall back upon such a theory as this...Let us get a firm grip of the very little which we do know, so that when fresh facts arise we may be ready to fit them into their places. I take it, in the first place, that neither of us is prepared to admit diabolical intrusions into the affairs of men. Let us begin by ruling that entirely out of our minds."
(Holmes; *The Devil's Foot*)

I have investigated many crimes, but I have never yet seen one which was committed by a flying creature. As long as the criminal remains upon two legs so long must there be some indentation, some abrasion, some trifling displacement which can be detected by the scientific searcher. (Holmes; *Black Peter*)

"They are singular, not to say grotesque...May I ask whether the two busts smashed in Dr. Barnicot's rooms were the exact duplicates of the one which was destroyed in Morse Hudson's shop?" (Holmes)
"They were taken from the same mould."
"Such a fact must tell against the theory that the man who breaks them is influenced by any general hatred of Napoleon. Considering how many hundreds of statues of the great Emperor must exist in London, it is too much to suppose such a coincidence as that a promiscuous iconoclast should chance to begin upon

three specimens of the same bust." (Holmes; *Charles Augustus Milverton*)

*That process...starts upon the supposition that when you have eliminated all which is impossible, then whatever remains, however improbable, must be the truth. It may well be that several explanations remain, in which case one tries test after test until one or other of them has a convincing amount of support.* (Holmes; *The Blanched Soldier*)

*As it was first presented to me, there were three possible explanations... There was the explanation that...Once again I could not get the theory to fit the fact...There remained the third possibility, into which, rare and unlikely as it was, everything seemed to fit.* (Holmes; *The Blanched Soldier*)

*There is only one possible way...We must fall back upon the old axiom that when all other contingencies fail, whatever remains, however improbable, must be the truth. Here all other contingencies have failed.* (Holmes; *The Bruce-Partington Plans*)

*That is the case as it appears to the police, and improbable as it is, all other explanations are more improbable still.* (Holmes; *Silver Blaze*)

*There is no great mystery in this matter...the facts appear to admit of only one explanation.* (Holmes; *The Sign of the Four*)

*It is the only hypothesis which covers the facts.* (Holmes; *The Sign of the Four*)

Assume a crime has taken place and we are faced with the problem of how the criminal escaped from a locked room. Sometimes we need to think the other way around. The question is not how the criminal escaped but how he got into the room in the first place. Sometimes one problem solves the other.

**TEST OUR THEORY– if it disagrees with the facts it is wrong**

*Physicians often pride themselves on curing all their patients with a remedy that they use. But the first thing to ask them is whether they have tried doing nothing, i.e., not treating other patients; for how can they otherwise know whether the remedy or nature cured them?* (Claude Bernard)

*These deductions, gentlemen, must however be confirmed by absolute and concrete evidence...Never neglect to ratify your deductions.* (Joseph Bell; *Dr. Joe Bell*)

*To choose a road, to stop habitually and to ask whether you have not gone astray, that is the true method.* (Louis Pasteur)

*"You suspect someone?"*
*"I suspect myself."* (Holmes)
*"What!"*
*"Of coming to conclusions too rapidly."*
*"Then go to London and test your conclusions."*
*"Your advice is very excellent. Miss Harrison." said Holmes rising. "I think, Watson, we cannot do better. Do not allow yourself to indulge in false hopes, Mr. Phelps. The affair is a very tangled one."* (The Naval Treaty)

*"Do you see any clue?"*
*"You have furnished me with seven, but of course I must test them before I can pronounce upon their value."* (Holmes; *The Naval Treaty*)

*I am inclined to...test one or two theories which I have formed.* (Holmes; *The Solitary Cyclist*)

*I think that there is a small experiment which we may try tomorrow, Watson, in order to throw some light on the matter.* (Holmes; *Shoscombe Old Place*)

*"I have no doubt that you have hit upon the truth."*
*"It will be verified or disproved at the trial."* (Holmes; *The Empty House*)

*It has been a case for intellectual deduction, but when this original intellectual deduction is confirmed point by point by quite a number of independent incidents, then the subjective becomes objective and we can say confidently that we have reached our goal. I had, in fact, reached it before we left Baker Street, and the rest has merely been observation and confirmation.* (Holmes; *The Sussex Vampire*)

*If the fresh facts which come to our knowledge all fit themselves into the scheme, then our hypothesis may gradually become a solution.* (Holmes; *Wisteria Lodge*)

*Does your explanation cover every point?* (Holmes; *The Priory School*)

*I have forged and tested every link of my chain, Professor Coram, and I am sure that it is sound.* (Holmes; *The Golden Pince-Nez*)

*Every link is now in its place and the chain is complete.* (Holmes; *Thor Bridge*)

**Facts don't lie but we may have interpreted or stated them wrong and therefore drawn the wrong conclusion**
*"Holmes," I cried, "this is impossible."*
*"Admirable!"..."A most illuminating remark. It is impossible as I state it, and therefore I must in some respect have stated it wrong. Yet you saw for yourself."* (Holmes; *The Priory School*)

**Imagination has its value – It may have been impossible only because we didn't consider other possibilities**
*See the value of imagination...We imagined what might have happened, acted upon the supposition, and find ourselves justified.* (Holmes; *Silver Blaze*)

**Check for other possible explanations – What else can explain this?**
*Knowledge of pathological or abnormal conditions cannot be gained without previous knowledge of normal states...We cannot judge the influence of a remedy on the course and outcome of a disease if we do not previously know the natural course and outcome of the disease.* (Claude Bernard)

*There is nothing more deceptive than an obvious fact.* (Holmes; *The Boscombe Valley Mystery*)

*One should always look for a possible alternative and provide against it. It is the first rule of criminal investigation.* (Holmes; *Black Peter*)

*Life is infinitely stranger than anything which the mind of man could invent.* (Holmes; *A Case of Identity*)

*Well, there are alternative explanations.* (Holmes; *The Three Gables*)

*Have you any alternative theory which will meet the facts?* (Holmes; *The Sign of the Four*)

*There were three possible courses.* (Holmes; *The Hound of the Baskervilles*)

*When a fact appears to be opposed to a long train of deductions, it invariably proves to be capable of bearing some other interpretation.* (Holmes; *A Study in Scarlet*)

*It is a possibility and we cannot afford to disregard it.* (Holmes; *The Naval Treaty*)

*I don't mean to deny that the evidence is in some ways very strongly in favour of your theory...I only wish to point out that there are other theories possible.* (Inspector Lestrade; *The Norwood Builder)*

*Because we have in this case one singular incident coming close to the heels of another singular incident. The police are making the mistake of concentrating their attention upon the second, because it happens to be the one which is actually criminal. But it is evident to me that the logical way to approach the case is to begin by trying to throw some light upon the first incident -- the curious will, so suddenly made, and to so unexpected an heir. It may do something to simplify what followed.* (Holmes; *The Empty House*)

*We all learn by experience, and your lesson this time is that you should never lose sight of the alternative.* (Holmes; *Black Peter*)

*Let us weigh the one against the other.* (Holmes; *The Priory School*)

*"But what are your alternatives?"*
*"I could mention several. You must admit that it is curious and suggestive that this incident should occur on the eve of this important match, and should involve the only man whose presence seems essential to the success of the side. It may, of course, be coincidence, but it is interesting. Amateur sport is free from betting, but a good deal of outside betting goes on among the public, and it is possible that it might be worth someone's while to get at a player as the ruffians of the turf get at a race-horse. There is one explanation. A second very obvious one is that this young man really is the heir of a great property, however modest his means may at present be, and it is not impossible that a plot to hold him for ransom might be concocted."* (Holmes; *The Missing Three-Quarter*)

## On the other hand
*Yes...you have seen me miss my mark before, Watson. I have an instinct for such things, and yet it has sometimes played me false. It seemed a certainty when first it flashed across my mind in the cell at Winchester, but one drawback of an active mind is that one can always conceive alternative explanations which would make our scent a false one.* (Holmes; *Thor Bridge*)

**Patience – Take time to think things over**

*Sherlock Holmes was a man...who, when he had an unsolved problem upon his mind, would go for days, and even for a week, without rest, turning it over, rearranging his facts, looking at it from every point of view until he had either fathomed it or convinced himself that his data were insufficient.* (Dr. Watson; *The Man with the Twisted Lip*)

*With your permission, gentlemen, we will now return to our cottage, for I am not aware that any new factor is likely to come to our notice here. I will turn the facts over in my mind.* (Holmes; *The Devil's Foot*)

*I think I should like to sit quietly for a few minutes and think it out.* (Holmes; *Thor Bridge*)

*"I wish I knew how you reach your results."*
*"I reached this one...by sitting upon five pillows and consuming an ounce of shag."* (Holmes; *The Man with the Twisted Lip*)

*It is quite a three pipe problem, and I beg that you won't speak to me for fifty minutes.* (Holmes; *The Red-Headed League*)

*I knew that seclusion and solitude were very necessary for my friend in those hours of intense mental concentration during which he weighed every particle of evidence, constructed alternative theories, balanced one against the other, and made up his mind as to which points were essential and which immaterial.* (Dr. Watson; *The Hound of the Baskervilles*)

**And avoid distractions and concentrate on the problem**
*I am very busy just now, and I desire no distractions.* (Holmes; *The Three Students*)

*My friend, who loved above all things precision and concentration of thought, resented anything which distracted his attention from the matter in hand.* (Dr. Watson; *The Solitary Cyclist*)

*His mind was so absolutely concentrated upon the matter before him that a question or remark fell unheeded upon his ears, or, at the most, only provoked a quick, impatient snarl in reply...every one of his actions was directed towards a definite end.* (Dr. Watson; *The Boscombe Valley Mystery*)

*Holmes sat in silence in the cab as we drove back to Baker Street, and I knew from his drawn brows and keen face that his mind, like my own, was busy in endeavoring to frame some scheme into which all these strange and apparently disconnected episodes could be fitted.* (Dr. Watson; *The Hound of the Baskervilles*)

**And when we don't get anywhere – accept doing nothing and wait until more evidence is available.**
*Well, I think we had best let matters develop a little further until we have clearer data.* (Holmes; *The Three Gables*)

*And now, Doctor, we can do nothing until the answers to those letters come, so we may put our little problem upon the shelf for the interim.* (Holmes; *A Case of Identity*)

## Distance gives perspective – Sometimes we need to remove ourselves from the problem and get a fresh perspective

*One of the most remarkable characteristics of Sherlock Holmes was his power of throwing his brain out of action and switching all his thoughts on to lighter things whenever he had convinced himself that he could no longer work to advantage.* (Dr. Watson; *The Bruce-Partington Plans*)

*Now, my dear fellow, we can't help matter by making ourselves nervous about them, so let me implore you to go to bed and so be fresh for whatever may await us to-morrow.* (Holmes; *The Naval Treaty*)

*I gave my mind a thorough rest by plunging into a chemical analysis. One of our greatest statesmen has said that a change of work is the best rest. So it is. When I had succeeded in dissolving the hydrocarbon which I was at work at, I came back to our problem of the Sholtos, and thought the whole matter out again.* (Holmes; *The Sign of the Four*)

*Let us walk along the cliffs together and search for flint arrows. We are more likely to find them than clues to this problem. To let the brain work without sufficient material is like racing an engine. It racks itself to pieces. The sea air, sunshine, and patience, Watson--all else will come.* (Holmes; *The Devil's Foot*)

*Let us escape from this weary workaday world by the side door of music. Carina sings to-night at the Albert Hall, and we still have time to dress, dine, and enjoy.* (Holmes; *The Retired Colourman*)

*But if I had not taken things for granted, if I had examined everything with care which I should have shown had we approached the case DE NOVO and had no cut-and-dried story to warp my mind, should I not then have found something more definite to go upon? Of course I should.* (Holmes; *The Abbey Grange*)

## SOME OTHER TOOLS

### Put yourself in the other person's shoes
*Well, now, let us put ourselves in the place of Jonathan Small. Let us look at it from his point of view...Now what could Jonathan Small do?* (Holmes; *The Sign of the Four*)

*You'll get results, Inspector, by always putting yourself in the other fellow's place, and thinking what you would do yourself. It takes some imagination, but it pays.* (Holmes; *The Retired Colourman*)

*I put myself in the man's place and, having first gauged his intelligence, I try to imagine how I should myself have proceeded under the same circumstances.* (Holmes; *The Musgrave Ritual*)

*If you could for one moment put yourself in the place of this young man, would you choose the very night after the will had been made to commit your crime? Would it not seem dangerous to you to make so very close a relation between the two incidents? Again, would you choose an occasion when you are known to be in the house, when a servant has let you in? And, finally, would you take the great pains to conceal the body and yet leave your own stick as a sign that you were the criminal? Confess, Lestrade, that all this is very unlikely.* (Holmes; *The Norwood Builder*)

### It we could see the world the way others see it, we easier understand why they do what they do
*"His conduct was certainly not very gracious."*

"Ah, Watson...perhaps you would not be very gracious either, if, after all the trouble of wooing and wedding, you found yourself deprived in an instant of wife and of fortune. I think that we may judge Lord St. Simon very mercifully and thank our stars that we are never likely to find ourselves in the same position." (Holmes; *The Noble Bachelor*)

## Get a different view – talk it over with someone else
*There's plenty of thread, no doubt, but I can't get the end of it into my hand. Now, I'll state the case clearly and concisely to you, Watson, and maybe you can see a spark where all is dark to me.* (Holmes; *The Man with the Twisted Lip*)

*Nothing clears up a case so much as stating it to another person, and I can hardly expect your co-operation if I do not show you the position from which we start.* (Holmes; *Silver Blaze*)

*If you will find the facts, perhaps others may find the explanation.* (Holmes; *Thor Bridge*)

*I was a whetstone for his mind. I stimulated him. He liked to think aloud in my presence. His remarks could hardly be said to be made to me -- many of them would have been as appropriately addressed to his bedstead -- but none the less, having formed the habit, it had become in some way helpful that I should register and interject. If I irritated him by a certain methodical slowness in my mentality, that irritation served only to make his own flame-like intuitions and impressions flash up the more vividly and swiftly. Such was my humble role in our alliance.* (Dr. Watson; *The Creeping Man*)

*I am afraid, my dear Watson, that most of your conclusions were erroneous. When I said that you stimulated me I meant, to be frank, that in noting your fallacies I was occasionally guided towards the truth.* (Holmes; *The Hound of the Baskervilles*)

## Combine experiences
*There were two of us in the hunt, and when two men set out to find a golf ball in the rough, they expect to come across it were the straight line marked in their minds eye to it, from their original positions, crossed. In the same way, when two men set out to investigate a crime mystery, it is where their researches intersect that we have a result.* (Joseph Bell; *Dr. Joe Bell*)

*Now we will take another line of reasoning. When you follow two separate chains of thought, Watson, you will find some point of intersection which should approximate to the truth.* (Holmes; *The Disappearance of Lady Frances Carfax*)

*Oh, you must not let me influence you in any way! I suggest that you go on your line and I on mine. We can compare notes afterwards, and each will supplement the other.* (Holmes; *The Six Napoleons*)

*Our researches have evidently been running on parallel lines, and when we unite our results I expect we shall have a fairly full knowledge of the case.* (Holmes; *The Hound of the Baskervilles*)

## Don't make the world fit your tools and use the right tool for the job

*The advances on the laboratory side and the perfection of instruments have added much to our powers of diagnosis, but they have given some men the idea that they are everything and the use of one's eyes and hands is looked on as old-fashioned. The man whose first idea in an obscure thoracic case is to have an x-ray plate taken and who cannot "bother" with physical signs does not deserve the name diagnostician.* (Thomas McCrae; *The Method of Zadig*)

*To my mind accurate habits of working and thinking are a great safeguard against these supposed short cuts to diagnosis.* (Thomas McCrae; *The Method of Zadig*)

## A rule is only a rule if it's always true

*I never make exceptions. An exception disproves the rule.* (Holmes; *The Sign of the Four*)

## Watch out for overconfidence

*My case is, as I have told you, almost complete; but we must not err on the side of overconfidence. Simple as the case seems now, there may be something deeper underlying it.* (Holmes; *The Sign of the Four*)

*"What effect do you think it will have upon his plans now that he knows you are here?"*
*"It may cause him to be more cautious, or it may drive him to desperate measures at once. Like most clever criminals, he may be too confident in his own cleverness and imagine that he has completely deceived us."* (Holmes; *The Hound of the Baskervilles*)

*He felt so clever and so sure of himself that he imagined no one could touch him.* (Holmes; *The Retired Colorman)*

**Update our beliefs in light of new information**
*I have devised seven separate explanations, each of which would cover the facts as far as we know them. But which of these is correct can only be determined by the fresh information which we shall no doubt find waiting for us.* (Holmes; *The Copper Beeches*)

*Well, now, Watson, let us judge the situation by this new information.* (Holmes; *Wisteria Lodge*)

**Criticize ourselves – Have we tried to find evidence against what we believe? Why might we be wrong? What have we overlooked? What (new) information or evidence is needed to make us change our mind?**
*When we meet a fact which contradicts a prevailing theory, we must accept the fact and abandon the theory, even when the theory is supported by great names and generally accepted.* (Claude Bernard)

**When we get better understanding or the facts or evidence don't agree with the theory we must change the theory and change course**
*I have steadily endeavoured to keep my mind free so as to give up any hypothesis, however much beloved...as soon as facts are shown to be opposed to it.* (Charles Darwin)

*What do you think of my theory?...at least it covers all the facts. When new facts come to our knowledge which cannot be covered by it, it will be time enough to reconsider it.* (Holmes; *The Yellow Face*)

*I can only claim the merit that I instantly reconsidered my position when, however, it became clear to me that whatever danger threatened an occupant of the room could not come either from the window or the door.* (Holmes; *The Speckled Band*)

*Now, Count, you are a card-player. When the other fellow has all the trumps, it saves time to throw down your hand.* (Holmes; *The Mazarin Stone*)

## Sometimes mistakes are made
*Because I made a blunder, my dear Watson - which is, I am afraid, a more common occurrence than anyone would think who only knew me through your memoirs. The fact is that I could not believe it possible that the most remarkable horse in England could long remain concealed, especially in so sparsely inhabited a place as the north of Dartmoor.* (Holmes; *Silver Blaze*)

*I confess...that any theories which I had formed from the newspaper reports were entirely erroneous.* (Holmes; *Silver Blaze*)

*I ought to know by this time that when a fact appears to be opposed to a long train of deductions, it invariably proves to be capable of bearing some other interpretation.* (Holmes; *A Study in Scarlet*)

## Learn from your mistakes – and learn the general lessons

*Well, well, we can't expect to have it all our own way, Watson!* (Holmes; *The Six Napoleons*)

*Hum! It may prove the simplest matter in the world, but all the same at first glance this is just a little curious, is it not? A gang of burglars acting in the country might be expected to vary the scene of their operations, and not to crack two cribs in the same district within a few days. When you spoke last night of taking precautions I remember that it passed through my mind that this was probably the last parish in England to which the thief or thieves would be likely to turn their attention--which shows that I have still much to learn.* (Holmes; *The Reigate Squire*)

*If it should ever strike you that I am getting a little over-confident in my powers, or giving less pains to a case than it deserves, kindly whisper "Norbury" in my ear, and I shall be infinitely obliged to you.* (Holmes; *The Yellow Face*)

*Should you care to add the case to your annals, my dear Watson...it can only be as an example of that temporary eclipse to which even the best-balanced mind may be exposed. Such slips are common to all mortals, and the greatest is he who can recognize and repair them.* (Holmes; *The Disappearance of Lady Frances Carfax*)

*I confess that I have been as blind as a mole, but it is better to learn wisdom late than never to learn it at all.* (Holmes; *The Man with the Twisted Lip*)

*There must be an honest reckoning of our mistakes. No part of the training is more essential. We all know the man who has made an incorrect diagnosis, but who, before the operation or post mortem is over, has nearly convinced himself that he did make the correct diagnosis and before night is quite sure of it. For him no good has come from the lesson. To learn we must face the mistakes and try to find out why we made them. Then comes our gain.* (Thomas McCrae; *The Method of Zadig*)

*We should all have the desire to reduce our errors to the minimum and to eliminate entirely those due to careless observations and slovenly habits of thinking. To observe accurately, to reason clearly, to hold ourselves to as high a standard of efficiency as our equipment permits, are within the powers of all.* (Thomas McCrae; *The Method of Zadig*)

## It is easy to be wise after the event, but very difficult to be wiser

*It is easy to be wise after the event.* (Holmes; *Thor Bridge*)

*"How absurdly simple", I cried.*
*"Quite so...Every problem becomes very childish when once it is explained to you."* (Holmes; *The Dancing Men*)

*A patient dies in whom you have made a diagnosis of typhoid fever, and at autopsy military tuberculosis is found. You are wise after the event but the laboratory Diener or a first year student is just as wise as you. To be wiser, or in other words to lessen the chance of your making the same mistake again, is quite another matter. You will certainly be no wiser if you have persuaded yourself that after all you did think it was military tuberculosis. For one's own training it is better to make an incorrect diagnosis than none at all-if you call yourself to account afterwards.* (Thomas McCrae; *The Method of Zadig*)

## SOME OTHER LESSONS
### Know our limitations
*The best physician is the most conscious of the limitations of his art.* (Benjamin Jowett)

*The best part of our knowledge is that which teaches us where knowledge leaves off and ignorance begins. Nothing more clearly separates a vulgar from a superior mind, than the confusion in the first between the little that it truly knows, on the one hand, and what it half knows and what it thinks it knows on the other.* (Oliver Wendell Holmes)

### Do we really have an important case? Deal with things that really matter and that we can do something about
*We are not much better off to-night. Again, there was no direct connection between the hound and the man's death. We never saw the hound. We heard it, but we could not prove that it was running upon this man's trail. There is a complete absence of motive. No, my dear fellow; we must reconcile ourselves to the fact that we have no case at present, and that it is worth our while to run any risk in order to establish one.* (Holmes; The Hound of the Baskervilles)

*Now, Mr. Mac and you, Mr. White Mason, I wish to give you a very earnest piece of advice. When I went into this case with you I bargained, as you will no doubt remember, that I should not present you with half-proved theories, but that I should retain and work out my own ideas until I had satisfied myself that they were correct. For this reason I am not at the present moment telling you all that is in my mind. On the other* hand, I said that I would play the game fairly by you, and I do not think it is a fair game to allow you for one unnecessary moment to waste your energies upon a profitless task. Therefore I am here to advise you this morning, and my advice to you is summed up in three words -- abandon the case. (Holmes; *The Valley of Fear*)

## Don't think about how to get things done, instead ask whether they're worth doing in the first place

*He will hold a card back for years in order to play it at the moment when the stake is best worth winning.* (Holmes; *Charles Augustus Milverton*)

*You must play your cards as best you can when such a stake is on the table.* (Holmes; *Charles Augustus Milverton*)

## A lot of misery comes from what we allow ourselves to get dragged into

## Avoid danger – we shouldn't expect to survive when we enter tough seas

*It was a singular spot...that old death trap of sailing vessels, with its fringe of black cliffs and surge swept reefs on which innumerable seamen have met their end.* (Dr. Watson; *The Devil's Foot*)

*Meantime, lady...have a care! Have a care! You can't play with edged tools forever without cutting those dainty hands.* (Holmes; *The Three Gables*)

*"Danger is part of my trade..."* (Holmes)
*"That is not danger...It is inevitable destruction. You stand in the way not merely of an individual, but of a might organization, the full extent of which you, with all your cleverness, have been unable to realize. You must stand clear, Mr. Holmes, or be trodden under foot."* (Professor Moriarty; *The Final Problem*)

*Watson, to understand that I am by no means a nervous man. At the same time, it is stupidity rather than courage to refuse to recognize danger when it is close upon you.* (Holmes; *The Final Problem*)

**Learn to tell the lions from the lambs**

**Know your enemy – When you bargain with a fox, beware of tricks**
*"You have probably never heard of Professor Moriarty?"* (Holmes)
*"Never."*
*"Aye, there's the genius and the wonder of the thing!...The man pervades London, and no one has heard of him...His career has been an extraordinary one. He is a man of good birth and excellent education, endowed by nature with a phenomenal mathematical faculty...But the man had hereditary tendencies of the most diabolical kind. A criminal strain ran in his blood, which, instead of being modified, was increased and rendered infinitely more dangerous by his extraordinary mental powers...He is the Napoleon of crime, Watson. He is the organizer of half that is evil and of nearly all that is undetected in this great city. He is a genius, a philosopher, an abstract thinker. He has a brain of the first order."* (*The Final Problem*)

**We shouldn't disregard even a small probability**
*We have no right to take anything for granted...It is certainly ten to one that they go downstream, but we cannot be certain.* (Holmes; *The Sign of the Four*)

**The future is hard to predict – even for Holmes**
*It is a formidable difficulty, and I fear that you ask too much when you expect me to solve it. The past and the present are within the field of my inquiry, but what a man may do in the future is a hard question to answer.* (Holmes; *The Hound of the Baskervilles*)

**You know my methods. Apply them!** (Holmes; *The Hound of the Baskervilles*)

**BIBLIOGRAPHY**

Joseph Bell, "*Mr. Sherlock Holmes*"; published in *The Bookman*, reprinted in the introduction of *A Study in Scarlet*, London: Ward, Lock & Bowden Limited, 1894, RBC Call No. Cameron 2A.5

Claude Bernard, *An Introduction to the Study of Experimental Medicine*; Dover Publications, Inc., 1957

Arthur Conan Doyle, *The Original Illustrated Sherlock Holmes*; Castle Books, New York

Arthur Conan Doyle, *Sir Arthur Conan Doyle: Memories and Adventures*; Wordsworth Ed. Ltd, 2007

R. Austin Freeman, *The Red Thumb Mark*; Wildside Press, LLC., 2005

R. Austin Freeman, *The Penrose Mystery*; Stratus Books Ltd., Cornwall, UK, 2008

Martin Gardner, *The Relativity Explosion*; New York: Vintage Books, 1976

Oliver Wendell Holmes, Sr. *Medical Essays;* www.gutenberg.net, 2006

Ely Liebow, *Dr. Joe Bell: Model for Sherlock Holmes*; Popular Press, 2007

James Alexander Lindsay, *Medical Axioms, Aphorisms, and Clinical Memoranda*; H.K. Lewis & Co. Ltd., 1923

Thomas McCrae, *The Method of Zadig in the Practise of Medicine;* Canadian Medical Association Journal, 1914 July; 4(7): 577–588

Michel de Montaigne, *The Complete Essays*; translated by M.A. Screech, Penguin Books, Ltd, London, 1987, 1991, 2003

Edgar Allan Poe, *The First Detective: The Complete Auguste Dupin Stories;* Leonaur Ltd, 2009

Jessie Saxby, *Joseph Bell: An Appreciation by an Old Friend*; Edinburgh, Oliphant, Anderson & Ferrier, 1913

Daniel Stashower, *Teller of Tales: The Life of Arthur Conan Doyle*; Henry Holt and Company, 1999

Many more novels, novellas, ebooks, travel guides, and biographies from the world's leading Sherlock Holmes publishers.

www.mxpublishing.com

www.mxpublishing.co.uk

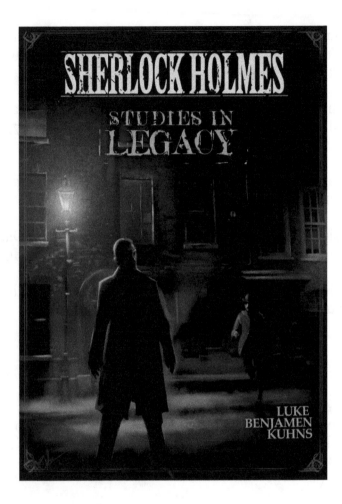

Sherlock Holmes – Studies in Legacy.

The Untold Adventures of Sherlock Holmes Volume 2

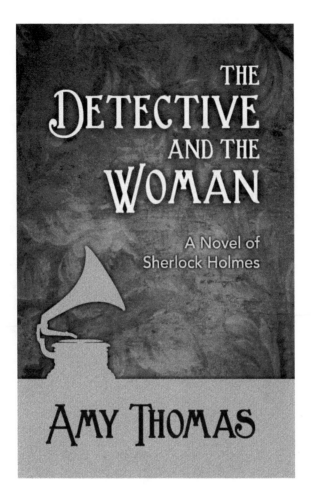

The Detective and The Woman and the new sequel, The Detective
The Woman and The Winking Tree

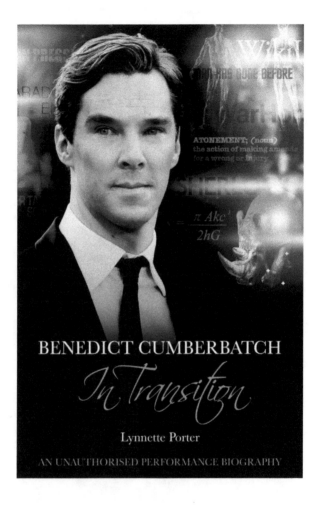

Benedict Cumberbatch, In Transition

The definitive performance biography.

Holmes and Watson are sent to Russia on their most dangerous
mission ever.

www.mxpublishing.com

CPSIA information can be obtained
at www.ICGtesting.com
Printed in the USA
BVHW040347160223
658587BV00003B/241